Tommy's Lost Shell

Pam Chapman

illustrated by Marjory Gardner

Modern Curriculum Press

Cleveland and Toronto

Tommy Turtle lived next to a swamp.

2

One day when he came back from a walk,
something was missing.

He had lost his shell.

He found a hat...

4

but that was too floppy.

He found a lunchbox…

but that was too square.

He found a button...

but that was too small.

He found a lid...

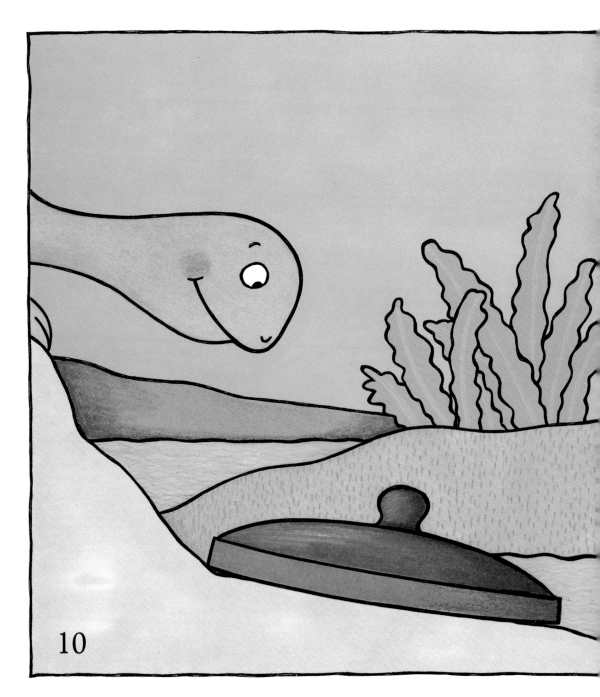

but that was too flat.

He found an egg carton…

12

but that was too bumpy.

Then, under a bush, he saw something.

It was round and brown and scaly.

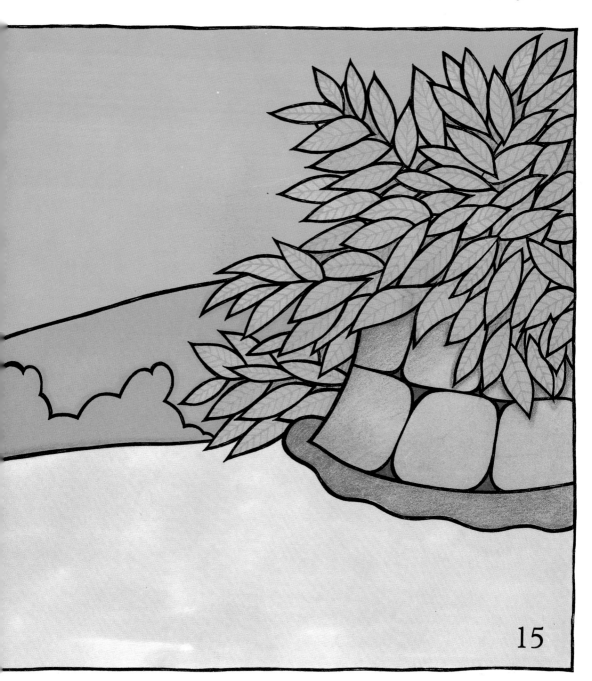

He tried it on...

and it was just right.